Shadow Stallion

JOLLY
FiSH
PRESS
Mendota Heights, Minnesota

By Whitney Sanderson
Illustrated by Jomike Tejido

Book design by Sarah Taplin
Illustrations by Jomike Tejido
Illustrations on pages 8, 9, 14, 31, 51 by North Star Editions

Published in the United States by Jolly Fish Press, an imprint of North Star Editions, Inc.

First Edition
First Printing, 2020

This is a work of fiction. Names, characters, places, and incidents are either the product of the author's imagination or are used fictitiously, and any resemblance to actual persons living or dead, business establishments, events, or locales is entirely coincidental.

Library of Congress Cataloging-in-Publication Data (pending)
978-1-63163-509-0 (paperback)
978-1-63163-508-3 (hardcover)

Jolly Fish Press
North Star Editions, Inc.
2297 Waters Drive
Mendota Heights, MN 55120
www.jollyfishpress.com

Printed in the United States of America

TABLE OF CONTENTS

Welcome to Summerville
Home of Magic Moon Stable

Unicorn Guardians

A long time ago, unicorns and people lived together. When people started hunting the unicorns, two girls decided to help. They used unicorn magic to create a powerful spell. It closed off the Enchanted Realm from the rest of the world. Only the girls' keys could open the Magic Gate.

When the girls grew up, they gave the keys to their daughters. Since then, two young girls have always been the Unicorn Guardians.

CHAPTER 1

Symbol Ceremony

Iris opened the *Book of Unicorns*. The full moon shone down on the page. Starsong and Heart's Mirror watched Iris curiously.

The foals were twins. Their mother was Heartsong. She stood to one side of the foals. Like all grown-up unicorns, Heartsong had a symbol beneath her horn. It was a music note inside a heart.

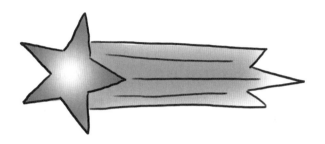

Starfire was the foals' father. He stood on their other side. His symbol was a shooting star. Starsong and Heart's Mirror had been born without symbols on their foreheads. But that was about to change.

"Is it time?" Ruby asked. She peered over Iris's shoulder. "Are you sure we have the right day?"

Iris nodded. "The book says that the Symbol Ceremony should happen during the first full moon after the foals are weaned. We saw them eating grass instead of nursing. So they must be ready."

Iris and Ruby were the Unicorn Guardians. The *Book of Unicorns* was a record kept by Guardians before them.

It was very old. It had advice that helped them care for the unicorn herd in the Enchanted Realm.

Now they both read aloud from the page:

"Two Guardians named these unicorns,

Looked after them since they were born.

Their time for growing up is here.

Now let these foals' true signs appear."

Iris and Ruby held up their keys to the Enchanted Realm. Beams of light shot out of the keys.

At the same time, light shone from

Heartsong's and Starfire's horns.

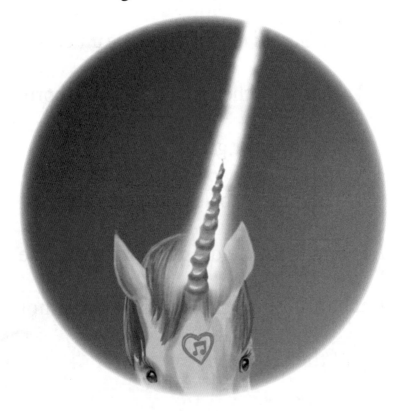

The beams of light arced through the air. They landed on the foals' foreheads.

The light was so bright that Iris had to close her eyes. When she opened them, new symbols had appeared beneath the foals' horns.

Starsong had three tiny silver stars. Heart's Mirror had two identical hearts mirroring each other.

"They're perfect," Ruby said. She went

over and hugged the foals.

Iris remembered when Starsong and Heart's Mirror had been born. She and Ruby had rescued them from danger in the Fairy Forest.

Iris looked over at the dark forest beyond the meadow. Her eyes widened in surprise.

A unicorn was standing between two tall trees. Or was it a unicorn?

It was black, with glowing red eyes. It had wings like a dragon's.

"Ruby, look," Iris said.

But Ruby was still paying attention to the foals. Iris tugged on her sleeve.

"Look!" she said again.

Ruby turned as Iris pointed toward the Fairy Forest.

But nothing was there.

CHAPTER 2

Legend of the Dragon Moon

Iris could not sleep that night. She was thinking about the strange unicorn she had seen. She had never heard of a unicorn with wings before. Or a unicorn with red eyes.

"Maybe you imagined it," Ruby had said. "Sometimes the trees in the forest look like strange creatures."

Iris turned on the light next to her bed. She went to her bookshelf and pulled out the *Book of Unicorns*. She flipped through its pages. The book was so big that she had not read all of it.

A picture on one page caught her eye. It was a drawing of a black unicorn with wings. It was just like the one she had seen. Iris read the words beneath the picture.

Iris read out loud, "Once every thirteen years, the moon in the Enchanted Realm turns as red as flame. It is known as the Dragon Moon. A unicorn born on this day will have the marks of a dragon. It may have wings, scales, or the ability to breathe fire. This unicorn will be cast out from the herd. It will not be accepted by other unicorns or by dragons."

Iris closed the book. The story was just a legend. The book did not say that a unicorn had ever been born under the Dragon Moon. But what else could explain what she had seen?

The next morning, Iris went by herself to the Enchanted Realm. It was before sunrise. The unicorns were asleep. Iris walked over to the place where she had seen the strange unicorn.

At first, she saw only trees. Then she heard a rustling sound. The black unicorn stepped out of the woods.

It fanned out its wings when it saw her. Its red eyes flashed.

Iris froze. The unicorn stepped toward her. Iris did not know if she should run away.

The black unicorn was a stallion.

"I wonder what your name is," Iris said. Her voice shook a little. "You don't have a symbol, so maybe you don't have a name yet."

The unicorn's eyes seemed to burn brighter.

"You blend in with the shadows," Iris said. "Except for your eyes. They glow like embers. Do you like the name Ember Shadow?"

The unicorn bobbed his head.

Iris tried to remember the words from the Symbol Ceremony. She held up her key. She hoped this would work.

"One Guardian named this unicorn, looked after him," she said. "His time for growing up is here. Now let his true sign appear."

The unicorn's forehead began to glow.

A moment later, a symbol appeared. It

showed three glowing red sparks.

Slowly, Iris reached out her hand. Ember Shadow held still while she patted his nose. His fur felt hot under her fingers. He really was like a dragon. But he wasn't scary.

Iris heard an angry squeal. She turned and saw Starfire charging toward them. His horn was lowered. He was ready to attack!

Ember Shadow flapped his wings and rose into the air. He flew away over the Fairy Forest.

Starfire stopped and reared up on his hind legs. He looked proud that he had chased off the strange unicorn.

Iris wondered if she would ever see Ember Shadow again.

CHAPTER 3

Outcast

Iris walked through the shadowy forest.
She held a lavastone that Ruby had found
in the Fire Mountains. The stone was cool
to the touch, but it glowed like a burning
coal. It helped light the way.

Iris reached a clearing. A stream ran through it. Thick moss grew under her feet. She noticed a hollow in the ground. Something had been sleeping there.

Iris looked across the clearing. Glowing red eyes stared back at her. She almost dropped the lavastone.

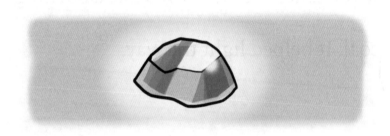

Ember Shadow stepped toward her. Iris's heart pounded. He was so big. His horn was so sharp. Maybe she should not have come here alone.

Ember Shadow stopped in front of her. He knelt down on one knee. He was inviting her to ride.

Iris felt like she was in a dream. She put the lavastone into her pocket. She climbed up onto Ember Shadow's back.

Ember Shadow gave his wings a few hard flaps. Suddenly, the ground was spinning away.

Ember Shadow carried Iris high into the night sky. The stars and moon seemed close enough to touch.

Ember Shadow flew over the Fairy Forest. Iris looked down at the trees.

Then Ember Shadow soared over the Fire Mountains. Iris could see into volcanoes filled with lava. She spotted dragon families in their caves on rocky ledges.

Ember Shadow turned back and flew over the meadow. The sleeping unicorns looked as small as Iris's model horses.

A ray of sunlight peeked over the horizon. The sky turned from dark blue to pale violet. Ember Shadow landed at the edge of the meadow. Iris slid down from his back.

"Thank you," she said. She stroked his neck. Smoke curled from his nostrils.

Iris felt sad when she thought about Ember Shadow living by himself in the forest. She was sure that he was lonely.

She looked over at the unicorn herd. The unicorns were now awake and grazing in the meadow.

"I wish you did not have to be an outcast," she said. "Maybe there is some way to make the other unicorns value you."

But when she turned back, Ember Shadow had already disappeared into the woods.

CHAPTER 4

Moonlight Meeting

Iris waited with Ember Shadow. They were in the clearing in the Fairy Forest. The moon was bright overhead. The stars shone.

A branch cracked in the woods. A moment later, Ruby appeared. She was riding Heartsong.

"Wow, he really does look like a dragon!" Ruby said.

Heartsong snorted in surprise when she spotted Ember Shadow. Her ears flattened back against her head. She was telling him to stay away.

"Do you have the apples?" Iris asked Ruby.

Ruby slid down from Heartsong's back. She held up a paper bag. Iris and Ruby reached into it. They each took out a yellow apple.

Heartsong sniffed the air. She flicked her tail. The apples were her favorite treat. They grew on trees that were too tall for the unicorns to reach themselves.

Ruby put her apple on the ground in front of Heartsong. The unicorn had to move closer to Ember Shadow to reach it.

Heartsong liked yellow apples more than she disliked Ember Shadow. She stepped forward and gobbled up the apple.

Iris set her apple down in front of Ember Shadow. But Ember Shadow stayed where he was. He was afraid to get closer to Heartsong.

But Heartsong saw the apple. She wanted it. She walked eagerly across the clearing.

Ember Shadow fluffed out his wings. He took a step back. Iris was afraid he might fly away again.

Heartsong stopped. She had noticed that Ember Shadow was afraid of her.

She lowered her head to the yellow apple on the ground. Instead of eating it, she nudged it with her nose. It rolled toward Ember Shadow.

He looked startled. But he slowly bent down and ate the apple.

When Ember Shadow lifted his head, Heartsong crossed her horn with his. Their horns made an X shape. That was how unicorns greeted each other when they wanted to be friends.

"What happened?" Ruby whispered to Iris. "I thought Heartsong was going to chase Ember Shadow away."

"Ember Shadow looks fierce, like a dragon," Iris said. "But he is more like a scared foal. Heartsong is a kind unicorn. I thought she might accept Ember Shadow if she got close enough to see his true nature."

"Do you think the other unicorns will be friends with him too?" Ruby asked.

"Let's find out," Iris said.

Ruby led Heartsong back toward the meadow. But Ember Shadow stayed where he was. His head hung low.

"You're coming with us this time," Iris said. She used the last apple in Ruby's bag to get him to follow her.

When they reached the meadow, Starfire came galloping over. He started to charge at Ember Shadow again.

Heartsong stepped between them and shook her head. She whinnied at Starfire. Then she stepped aside.

Iris held her breath. Ruby crossed her fingers.

This time, Ember Shadow stood his ground. Starfire tossed his head and stamped his hooves.

Heartsong whinnied at him again.

Then she went over to Ember Shadow

and stood beside him.

Starfire let out a snort. Then his whole body seemed to relax. He pranced forward and crossed horns with Ember Shadow, like Heartsong had done.

Iris and Ruby gave each other a high five.

One by one, the other unicorns came over. Some of them shied away when they saw Ember Shadow. But when they realized that Heartsong and Starfire had accepted him, they greeted him too.

Soon, Ember Shadow was grazing and playing with the herd. Starsong and Heart's Mirror started a game of tag with him.

They pranced on the ground. Ember

Shadow flew and soared above them.

When dawn came, Ember Shadow spread his wings and flew back into the Fairy Forest. The other unicorns continued to play without him.

"He must not like sunlight," Iris said.

"Some dragons only come out at night," Ruby said. "Maybe he's the same."

Ember Shadow was so different from other unicorns. But Iris knew that he would not be lonely anymore.

He could always come out of the shadows to visit his new friends.

THINK ABOUT IT

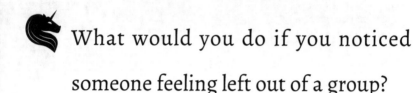 What would you do if you noticed someone feeling left out of a group?

Iris was scared of Ember Shadow at first. But she soon learned his true nature. Write about a time you learned something new or surprising about someone.

Iris and Ruby used apples to bring Heartsong and Ember Shadow together. What activities bring people together?

ABOUT THE AUTHOR

Whitney Sanderson grew up riding horses as a member of a 4-H club and competing in local jumping and dressage shows. She has written several books in the Horse Diaries chapter book series. She is also the author of *Horse Rescue: Treasure,* based on her time volunteering at an equine rescue farm. She lives in Massachusetts.

ABOUT THE ILLUSTRATOR

Jomike Tejido is an author and illustrator of the picture book *There Was an Old Woman Who Lived in a Book.* He also illustrated the Pet Charms and My Magical Friends leveled reader series. He has fond memories of horseback riding as a kid and has always loved drawing magical creatures. Jomike lives in Manila with his wife, two daughters, and a chow chow named Oso.

RETURN TO MAGIC MOON STABLE

Book 1

Book 2

Book 3

Book 4

Book 5

Book 6

Book 7

Book 8

AVAILABLE NOW